We All Rot Eventually

A horror Novella by

Mia Ballard

WE

ALL

ROT

EVENTUALLY

To LJ

One

The mini market gas station off the 405 smells like gasoline and burnt coffee, and it sticks to me like it knows I can't outrun it. The air breathes around me, alive in the way things you don't love are alive—buzzing, flickering, humming. The coolers whine in the corner. The lights pulse like they're thinking of dying. I lean on the counter, my chin resting on my palm, a bag of peach rings open beside me. The sugar clings to my fingers, melts into my skin, sticks to the parts of my thoughts I don't want to touch.

Outside, the parking lot stretches forever, endless as anything can be when it's full of strangers. Headlights smear across the glass, tracing shadows on the tile. Cars come and go, drivers passing like ghosts, their faces dissolving the second I try to catch them. I watch, but I'm not sure what I'm waiting for. Something. Someone. A feeling. It's the kind of ache that doesn't settle anywhere, just floats under your skin, making you itch.

The smell of gasoline is a second skin now. It soaks into my hair, my clothes, the spaces between my fingers. Sometimes, I wonder if I'd disappear without it. It clings to me like a memory I don't want to remember, like the day I came home from school when I was fourteen and my dad told me he was leaving my mom for another woman, or the way Ricky cried the night I told him I was leaving town and moving to L.A. and he said he would kill himself, but he didn't.

My phone sits on the counter flipped open, my face staring back at me, glossy and alive in a way I'm not. It's a photo from last summer, when I first arrived to
Los Angeles, back when I thought I'd have something by now. My lips are painted glittery pink, my hair falling perfectly pin straight, but the longer I stare, the less real it feels. I scroll through the rest from that day—my face again and again, always trying to catch itself, like a dog chasing its tail. It feels like looking at someone I used to know.

Tomorrow, I tell myself. Tomorrow will change everything. Tomorrow is the callback, and the callback means the movie, and the movie means *the life*. It means not standing under these lights, not smelling like cigars and gas and cheap hot dogs, not being the girl behind the counter. It means people saying my name like it means something, saying it with reverence, like a secret they get to hold in their mouths. But the name they'll call me tomorrow isn't even mine.

I gave it to myself one night when I couldn't stand being the girl I'd been anymore. It came out of me like a song I already knew the words to, something sharp and bright; *Alexa Valentine*. It sounded like a dare when I said it, like the name belonged to a girl with lips as red as stop signs, a girl people would crash their cars for. It sounded like it belonged to me, even though it didn't. Not yet.

Who I was before doesn't matter. Maybe she's still out there, some shadow of me walking barefoot in the fields I left behind, a girl with skinned knees and a bad temper, kicking sand in her crush's eyes in the first-grade because she wanted to see what rage looked like on someone else. Or maybe she died the night I told the devil what I wanted, her body sinking into the floorboards, her hands still clenched into fists.

A car pulls into the lot, its headlights catching me in the glass. For a second, I see myself—not the girl in the phone or the girl I show the customers, but someone softer, blurrier, slipping like smoke out of her own skin. Then the car parks, and the moment breaks. The lights buzz overhead. The smell of gas curls tighter around me. And I'm still here, beaming and restless, waiting for something I don't have a name for.

Two

My walk home is a slow dissolve through flickering shadows, past cars that might stop for me, past songs bleeding out of cracked windows, the kind of music that feels like the end of something. I wish I had a car but my little beat up 2001 Honda barely survived the drive across country to Los Angeles from Illinois. It only lasted a month more before breaking down completely and bursting into flames on the 405.

When I get home, the house smells like cigarettes and cheap ramen, the kind of smell that sticks to the drywall no matter how many windows you open. My roommates are scattered through the living room like they've been left there by a storm. There's Milo, aspiring screenwriter and our resident flaming gay, sprawled on the couch, chewing on his pen cap like he's trying to eat his own thoughts. He's writing a manifesto, or a screenplay, or maybe just a list of reasons he thinks the CIA is controlling the weather. I stopped asking after the night he showed me his "proof" in the form of Polaroids of chemtrails.

Then there's Danielle, standing by the window in one of her vintage nightgowns, the sheer fabric lit up by the glow of the streetlights. She's holding a glass of something brown and strong, pretending to read a book. Danielle is small and stacked, with platinum blonde hair and a perpetual duck face; she's the kind of girl who gets bored if people don't look at her, so she creates emergencies. Last week, she "accidentally" started a fire in the kitchen while trying to make crème brûlée, and two days later she asked if I thought she'd make a good arsonist. She wrote a letter to Charlie Manson last month. She's still waiting on a response.

And finally, there's Dave, slumped in the armchair, flipping through a crumpled copy of *Maxim* like it's holy scripture. I don't know why he lives here. None of us do. He showed up one day with a duffel bag and a blank stare, and Milo let him stay because, in his words, "Dave has the aura of someone who's seen a dead body." I'm pretty sure Dave is a pedophile. He only talks about movies with kids in them, and not in the normal way, but in a way that makes everyone else go quiet when he opens his mouth. But rent's due, and no one's brave enough to kick him out. Plus since it's Danielle's house, a gift from her rich parents who work in big tech and spend their holidays in the Caymans; she gets the last say, and she says the brooding (alleged) pedo can stay.

I wave at them on my way through the room, and Danielle raises her glass without looking up from her book. "How was the glamorous world of Mini Mart?" she asks.

"Unreal," I reply, and head down the hall before anyone can ask me about tomorrow.

My room is small and bare except for a futon that can switch from couch to bed in one swift pull, a thrifted full-length mirror, a clothing rack of all my cutest and sluttiest clothes, and the stacks of scripts I've been picking through like lottery tickets. A bunch of posters haphazardly plastered up on all my walls. There's a poster of Aaron Carter right above my futon bed. Poor boy has seen a lot of unholy things. I painted all the walls arsenic green a few weeks ago. Jury is still out if that was a good idea or not.

I sit cross-legged on the floor and pull tomorrow's lines out of my bag, smoothing the paper against my thigh. It's an indie movie called *Lovers in Dusk,* one of those quiet, weird ones with no clear plot and a lot of staring out of windows. I read the lines out loud, trying to find the girl in them, the one I'm supposed to be. She's angry and lonely and looking for something she can't quite name, and I think, *God, that's me, isn't it?*

An hour later, I'm restless, so I call Lars. He picks up on the first ring, like he always does, his voice smooth and sticky, like butter melting over something fried. Lars is an actor, too, though his IMDb page is more B-movie actor who dies during the first fifteen minutes than indie darling. He also plays the bass in an indie band that was mediocre at best. He looks like Keanu Reeves if Keanu Reeves had spent a summer in Daytona Beach and never left all floppy dark hair and tired eyes and deep tan lines he probably shouldn't still have in the fall. He always speaks like he has a point to prove, all loud with big gestures and exclamation points, and I don't love him, but I like the way he looks stretched out on my futon bed, his shirt half-buttoned, his smile lazy.

When he shows up, he smells like the inside of a hot car—leather and sweat and something metallic I can't place. He grins at me, tosses his leather jacket on my floor, and pulls a bag of coke out of his pocket like he's a magician revealing a dove. "You look tense," he says, shaking the bag like it was candy.

"I have a callback tomorrow," I say, sitting cross-legged on the futon.

"Even better," he says. He grabs a crumpled *People Magazine* from my nightstand, flipping through it until he lands on Jessica Simpson's face. He lays it flat on the floor, his movements quick, and dumps a line of coke right across Jessica's smile.

"Should I feel bad about this?" he asks, glancing up at me.

"No I really don't think she minds at all."

Lars snorts the line, his head snapping back like he's been hit by lightning. "Not bad," he says, grinning. "You want some?"

"No," I say, even though part of me does. I don't need it. I've already got the buzz of tomorrow in my veins, that slow, electric hum of possibility. But I watch him, the sharp curve of his jaw, the little flash of his tongue over his teeth. He's pretty, and he's fun, and tonight, that feels like enough.

The magazine crinkles as he brushes it aside, and Jessica's face disappears under the bed. I lie back on the futon, the script still crumpled in my hand, and Lars lies down next to me, his breath warm on my shoulder. The lights outside flicker, the city groaning with its own dreams, and for a moment, I think maybe this could be everything. But only for a moment.

Three

The room feels darker when Lars leaves around five in the morning, though it's probably just me. The full-length mirror catches me from across the room, that warped little thing I bought for ten bucks at a garage sale in Echo Park, and I can't help but look. I always look. My reflection feels like a stranger who keeps asking for things I can't give.

I've lost ten pounds this month. Maybe more. The scale stopped working last week, and I haven't replaced it. I don't need to. I know what it says when I look at my thighs, at my collarbones pressing sharp against my skin, at the way my face looks smaller now, prettier somehow, like the bones are trying to break through. But it's not enough. I suck in my stomach, tilt my chin. It's never enough.

Everyone says I'm beautiful. They've said it my whole life, like it's this fact they've all agreed on. My mom used to tell me, *You got lucky, mija.* And I am lucky. I know that. My dark hair falls perfectly without me trying, my skin glows like I've been dipped in gold, my features sharp but soft, like something carved to be admired but not touched. My mother was Cuban, my father Black, and I look like a memory of both, something bigger than myself. But even when people stare too long, even when I see them whispering about me behind their hands, I still feel like they're seeing something I can't.

I sleep for three hours, or maybe I don't sleep at all. My body is vibrating, my chest tight, the energy coiling in my stomach like something alive. The callback is at nine a.m., and I walk there because I don't trust the bus to get me there on time. The city is different in the morning; quieter, like it hasn't decided what kind of day it wants to have. My breath fogs up the air even though it's not cold, and I'm chewing gum because it feels like I need to keep my jaw moving or I might shatter from the tension.

The casting office is in one of those beige buildings that looks like it should belong to a dentist or a divorce lawyer. The elevator smells like tanning lotion and perfume, and I press the button for the third floor with my knuckle because I don't want to risk breaking my nail. When the doors open, I step into a hallway full of other girls, all of them thin and glowing and tall, all of them wearing that same look I see in my mirror: desperate but trying to hide it.

They don't say anything to me, but their eyes flick over my body, up and down, weighing me, measuring me. I glance at one of them—a blonde, bright and sharp like a knife—and she gives me a little smile, but it's not kind. It's the kind of smile you give a girl you think you're better than. I go into a dark corner and change out of my converse and into my black patent leather pumps. I'm wearing a short black dress that I know I look good in. I sit there and rehearse my lines, smearing bubblegum pink gloss on my lips every fifteen minutes until my name is finally called two hours later.

Inside the room, the casting director is sitting behind a long table, her hair slicked back, her glasses hanging off the edge of her nose. There are three other people with her, their faces unreadable, their pens tapping against their clipboards like they're keeping time. The space is cavernous, a weird mix of clinical and theatrical, and it makes my skin itch.

"Alexa Valentine," she says, and hearing my name like that—my name, the one I made—makes something tighten in my chest. I smile, wide but not too wide, and step to the center of the room.

The scene is simple. It's one of those quiet, heavy moments, all silence and stolen glances, the kind of thing you have to carry with your face and nothing else. I read the lines like I've practiced them a hundred times, but halfway through, I feel my hands start to tremble. My voice cracks on the last line, just a little, and for a second, I swear the director's mouth twitches like she might say something. But she doesn't.

They thank me when I'm done, and I walk out as slowly as I can without looking hesitant, my shoes clicking against the tile. The moment I step into the hallway, I feel like I can breathe again, but it's a shallow breath, not enough to fill my lungs. I change back into my converse and try to steady my hands as I tie the laces.

I don't know how I did. I don't know if it was good or bad or just forgettable, but I know that if I don't get this, I don't know what comes next. I press my back against the wall outside the building and stare up at the sky, the sunlight slicing through my vision like it's trying to hurt me. All I can think is, *I've lost ten pounds this month, and I'm still not enough.*

Four

When I get home, the house is holding its breath. The door creaks when I push it open, and the air is warm with too many bodies, too much talking, too much smoke. They're all at the table, all three of them—Milo hunched over his notebook, Danielle draped over the chair like she's in a photoshoot, Dave staring at something invisible, his fingers pressed into the wood grain.

Their heads turn when I step inside, all three at once, like a pack of animals. I drop my Gucci bag that I stole from my stepmom when I was sixteen by the door, feel their eyes on me as I pull off my jacket. My skin is tight, my hands still shaking, the humiliation of the callback sticking to me like a film I can't scrub off.

I walk into the room, trying to look calm, trying not to let it show. They're waiting for me to say something, but I don't know what they want. There's an open bottle of vodka on the table and a giant bowl of pesto bowtie pasta that no one offers me because they know I'll just throw it up later. Danielle is swirling her wine glass like she's bored already, her nails clinking against the glass.

I sit down, pick up the nearest cup, and pour myself something strong. The burn steadies me, just a little. The silence is taut and heavy, and I know they want me to fill it, so I do. "It didn't go well," I say, the words flat, clipped.

Danielle exhales smoke, her lips curling around a smirk. Milo flips a page in his notebook. Dave doesn't move. No one says anything, and I don't know if that's better or worse than whatever they're thinking.

I drink faster than I mean to, the vodka sliding warm into my stomach, spreading out like it's trying to soften me. The edges of the room blur, their voices circling, rising and falling, bits of their stories crashing into one another. Milo says something about a woman on the bus screaming that the world was ending. Danielle laughs, low and sharp, says something about a guy who offered her $1,000 to step on his face.

Dave doesn't speak until the vodka is gone. His voice cuts through the air like a blade, low and flat and heavier than the rest of ours. "Do you know what's on the dark web?" he asks.

Danielle snorts, and Milo sighs, but I feel the question stick, jagged and strange. I feel it sit in my chest, blooming.

Dave's voice doesn't waver. "Everything you can't get here."

Danielle stubs out her cigarette, her mouth twitching. "Like what? Cannibal recipes? Child porn? Be serious."

But I can't stop thinking about it, about the word *everything*. I can feel the vodka now, humming in my blood, loosening my body, opening something in me. I think about the audition, the way the casting director didn't even look at me, like I was already gone. I think about all the girls in the hallway, their perfect faces, their tight jeans, their hair catching the light like they'd rehearsed even that.

I don't say anything. I don't laugh. I don't meet anyone's eyes. The vodka keeps me warm, and the room is too loud, too thick with smoke and heat, and Dave's words hang in the air like something alive.

By the time I stand up, the room is a blur, my legs heavy, my stomach churning. Milo doesn't look up from his notebook. Danielle doesn't bother saying goodnight. Dave's eyes flicker to me for just a second, something unreadable behind them, but I don't meet his gaze.

When I close the door to my room, the word is still there, rattling in my head like a loose tooth. I lie on the futon, staring at the ceiling, the lights from outside carving strange shapes into the walls. My chest feels tight, and my hands won't stop shaking. I think about the callback. I think about everything I want and everything I don't have and how maybe I don't have to keep waiting for it.

Five

The bus smells like damp vinyl and something faintly chemical, like every bad decision ever made in a moving vehicle has been compressed into the seats and walls. My legs stick to the plastic, my heels digging into the rubber floor with each jolt forward, each stop that lets in a gust of warm, city-stained air. I'm overdressed for this bus at this hour, the kind of overdressed that gets you stares—my denim mini skirt hiked halfway up my thighs, my six-inch heels wobbling under me every time the driver slams the brakes. The guy three rows over is watching me like he paid for it, and I wonder if I should be flattered or just disgusted.

Danielle was supposed to be here. She's always here for these things, these shows, these nights spent pretending I'm there to support Lars when really I'm there to be noticed. But an hour ago, she texted me: *This guy wants me to peg him. Can't miss that opportunity.*

And because it's Danielle, and because there's nothing she wouldn't do for a story, I knew she meant it. So now it's just me, alone on the bus at 10 p.m., on my way to Lars' show, dressed like bait, because my roommate is pegging some guy and probably making a meal out of it.

The city moves past the window, all red light and half-sounds, the streets blurry under a sky so empty it might as well be another ceiling. I lean against the glass, my reflection hazy, almost beautiful if I tilt my head just right. I do this on purpose—these little outfits, these nights, these heels that wreck my arches and make me feel taller, better, less invisible. I do this because I still think it's possible to be discovered. That I'll show up in the corner of some shitty bar, and someone important will see me, see *something* in me. It's embarrassing, I know. But it's also the only thing keeping me moving.

The bus jolts to a stop, and I step off, my ankles bending in a way that feels unforgivable. The street smells like stale beer and car exhaust, the neon from the bar's sign buzzing faintly in the corner of my eye. It's not far—a hole-in-the-wall venue pretending to be grunge, the kind of place where you can't tell if the bathrooms are broken or just never worked to begin with.

Inside, it's loud. So loud it feels physical, the bass vibrating through my body, shaking loose the last shreds of self-awareness I brought with me. Lars is already onstage, a guitar slung low on his hips, his hair falling into his face. He's wearing his leather jacket, the one with the sleeves too short, and his mouth is open, his head tilted back, like he's in love with the sound coming out of him.

I stand in the back, leaning against the wall, my drink cold and sticky in my hand. Lars' band, *Stupid is As Stupid Does* is loud and careless, covering songs they don't have the range for, but Lars looks good—he always looks good—and I like the way his body moves under the lights. He catches my eye in the middle of a song, his grin slow and smug, and I know it's for me. That grin that says he already knows I'll go home with him tonight, even though we both know it doesn't mean anything.

I tell myself I'm not here for him. Not really. I'm here for the off-chance, for the possibility of a casting director or an indie filmmaker in the crowd, for someone who'll see me standing there, luminous and untouchable, and think, *yes, her.* But it's hard to hold onto that fantasy when Lars looks at me like I'm the only person in the room, when he smiles like he knows how this night ends.

When the set is over, I step outside for air. The street is quieter now, the neon light from the sign casting red streaks over the pavement. I light a cigarette, even though I don't smoke nicotine, holding it between my fingers like an accessory, like something to keep me steady. The smoke curls around my face, and I exhale slowly, watching it disappear into the night.

Lars comes out a few minutes later, his hair sticking to his forehead, his face flushed. He leans against the wall next to me, close enough that I can feel the heat of him. He's still buzzing from the set, talking fast about the crowd, about how the energy was *so good,* but I barely hear him. I'm staring at the street, at the glow of the neon, at the cigarette burning down between my fingers.

He kisses me then, his mouth tasting like beer and sweat, and I let him. I let him because it's easier than thinking, easier than admitting that we are not soulmates and he is not my person. His hands slide around my waist, pulling me closer, and for a moment, I let myself sink into it, into him, into the heat and the noise and the way he touches me in ways that make me weak.

But then the moment passes, and I pull back, my chest tight, my breath shallow. Lars doesn't say anything, just leans against the wall, his grin lazy and soft, and I wonder if he even notices the way my hands are shaking. He tells me he can't give me a ride home tonight and has to stay and shmooze but will come over later. Even though I'm not stoked at taking the bus home so late I shrug and say okay.

I stub out the cigarette on the curb, the smoke curling up one last time before it's gone. The city hums around us, and I think about the bus ride home, about the heels, about the fact that tomorrow is just another day of waiting to be seen. Lars is looking at me, but it's not enough. It never is.

Six

I wake up with his dick against my thigh. It's warm and soft, pressing into me like a small, lazy animal. The room is too hot, the light coming through the blinds in thick, syrupy streaks that land on my face, on his chest, on the pile of our clothes slumped in the corner. My mouth tastes like vodka and cigarettes, and I don't remember what time we fell asleep, or if I even did.

Lars is heavy against me, his arm thrown over my waist, his body cold. I push him, gently at first, then harder, rolling him onto his back so I can stretch out, but he doesn't move the way I expect. His body shifts with mine, but it's too limp, too slow. His arm flops against the mattress like a fish.

I blink at him, half-awake, waiting for him to make a sound, to grunt or mumble or pull me back against him, but his face doesn't change. His features are slack, his lips parted just enough to make him look dumb, his hair still falling into his eyes in a way that would've been sexy if I didn't suddenly feel like I couldn't breathe.

I push myself up on one elbow, staring at him. His skin looks strange. Pale, but not just pale—pale in a way that feels wrong, like the color has been drained out of him, like someone has pulled him out of the freezer.

"Lars," I say, but it comes out weak, my voice caught somewhere between curiosity and dread. I push at his shoulder again, harder this time, shaking him, but his head just rolls to the side, his hair sticking to his damp forehead.

My heart feels like it's dropped into my stomach. The room smells like sweat and stale alcohol, and I can hear my pulse pounding in my ears, loud and frantic. His chest isn't moving. I think, *maybe I'm wrong, maybe I'm still drunk, maybe this is just Lars being Lars.* But then I touch his face, and his skin is cold, not icy but cool in a way that makes my fingers curl back instinctively, like I've touched something that doesn't belong to me.

He's dead. I know it before I can admit it to myself, before the word even forms in my head. I sit there, staring at him, waiting for him to move, to cough, to laugh, to sit up and say something stupid about how I look like hell. But he doesn't. He just lies there, his body heavy and still, the room too quiet, too bright, too normal for what's happening.

I don't scream. I don't cry. I just sit there, my breath stuck in my throat, looking at Lars' face like I've never seen it before. Like he's a stranger, someone I've accidentally let into my bed, someone I don't know how to get rid of. I feel the sweat on my back, the ache in my legs, the faint stickiness of last night clinging to my skin, and all I can think is, *what now?*

Seven

After they cart Lars out, zipped into a bag that looks small for him, like they didn't account for the size of his limbs or the weight of his deadness, I sit on the curb with a scratchy blanket over my shoulders. I don't know who gave it to me, but it smells faintly like damp wool and something antiseptic, and I hold onto it because it's something to do with my hands. The street is crowded now—neighbors standing in clusters, watching the scene like they paid for tickets. The flashing lights of the ambulance paint their faces red, and I wonder if any of them are thinking about what it feels like to wake up next to a dead body.

Danielle is standing by the mailbox, her face blotchy, her eyes swollen like she's been crying for hours, though I know she hasn't. I had to call her, tell her to come back from wherever she was, tell her I *needed* her, because I couldn't do this alone. When she finally walked in, she took one look at me, still sitting on the futon next to Lars' body, shaking. The minute she sees us, she falls apart. She's always been better at feeling things than I am, better at knowing what to do with all that mess.

I don't feel much, not really. Not about Lars. It's not like I loved him. He was a pretty face and a warm body, someone to fill the silence, someone who made me feel less invisible for a few hours at a time. But when Danielle runs into my room, I put on my best performance. It was like flipping a switch. My voice broke at all the right moments, my knees hit the carpet like they'd rehearsed it, my face twisted into something fragile and wrecked. She didn't question it. She pulled me into her arms, her voice thick with panic, and I let myself cry against her shoulder, making all the right sounds, letting the sobs tear through me like they were mine.

And I haven't stopped since. Not because I feel anything, but because I know what's expected of me. The police ask me questions, and I answer them through tears, my voice trembling just enough to make them stop asking for a minute. Danielle hugs me by the mailbox, and I let myself collapse into her, burying my face in her hair, my shoulders shaking like I'm breaking in half.

The truth is, Lars has been dead for hours, and I still don't know how I'm supposed to feel about it. I should feel something. Guilt, sadness, anger. But all I feel is the faint hum of relief, the space he's left behind already filling with something else.

When the cops finally pull me into the car, Danielle is still crying, her mascara streaked down her face, her hands clinging to the edges of her sweater like they'll keep her upright. She tells me everything will be okay, that we'll get through this, that she's here for me, but I barely hear her. I nod, I sniffle, I touch her hand like it's a lifeline, but all I can think about is how easy it is to lie when no one is looking too closely.

In the back of the car, the blanket still draped over me, I stare at my knees, pale and bare, smudged with the remnants of Lars' sweat and my makeup. My hands feel too clean, too steady, resting in my lap, and I clench them into fists just to see if I can. I think about the morning, about how Lars looked in the light, pale and slack, his mouth open like he was about to tell me something stupid, like he wasn't already gone. I think about his hands, his long fingers curled against his stomach, and how I didn't want to touch him, not even to check if he was warm.

The car starts moving, and I lean my head against the window, watching the streetlights blur past. My face is still wet, my breathing still ragged, and I wonder how long I'll have to keep this up, how long I can make them believe that I'm wrecked, that I'm shattered, that I'm someone who cared enough to break.

Danielle waves as the car turns the corner, her hand trembling in the dark, and I wave back, slow and small, just enough to make it look real.

Eight

The knock is soft, hesitant, and I almost don't hear it over the buzz of the TV and the thick, low hum that's been building in my skull since the police dropped me off. I'm lying on the futon, the blanket from last night still wrapped around me, even though the room is too warm and smells like old sweat and stale vodka. My body feels stuck, my head heavy, my eyes burning from not enough sleep.

The knock comes again, just a little louder. Then, Milo's voice, flat and bored: "It's for you."

For a second, I don't move. I stare at the ceiling, at the yellowed patch of water damage that looks like an inkblot, my brain too slow to process what he means. The house phone hasn't rung in weeks. Maybe months. Nobody calls it except scam artists and debt collectors, and I don't know why anyone would be asking for me.

I sit up slowly, the blanket slipping off my shoulders, and Milo is standing in the doorway, holding the phone like it's something fragile. His shirt is wrinkled, his hair sticking up in places like he's been napping, and he looks at me with that faintly annoyed expression he always has, like he's the one being inconvenienced.

"It's for you," he says again, a little louder this time, and holds the phone out like it might bite him.

I furrow my brow, staring at it. "Who is it?"

He shrugs, shifting his weight onto one foot. "They said they're a producer."

I blink, my brain still catching up, my body already moving toward him. The phone is warm in my hand, slick with sweat from his fingers, and I press it to my ear slowly, like I'm afraid it's a trick. "Hello?"

The voice on the other end is crisp, polished, with that faintly detached cheerfulness that comes from someone who makes a lot of phone calls they don't really want to make. "Alexa Valentine?"

"Yes," I say, the word tight in my throat.

"This is Caroline Singer, one of the producers from *Lovers in the Dusk*. I wanted to call and let you know that we'd like to bring you back for a second round of auditions. Are you available tomorrow afternoon?"

My stomach flips, sharp and sudden, like I've stepped off a ledge I didn't know was there. I grip the phone tighter, my free hand curling into the blanket still draped over my lap. "Yes," I say quickly, my voice too loud, too eager. "Yes, I'm available."

"Great," she says, her tone smooth, professional. She gives me the time and the location, something about a casting office in Culver City, and I write it down on the back of an old McDonald's receipt I grab off the floor. When the call ends, the dial tone hums in my ear for a second before I lower the phone, staring at the smudged ink on the paper in my hand.

I sit there for a moment, the room spinning faintly around me. My body feels too big, my breath too loud, and all I can think about is how Lars' body looked yesterday morning, pale and slack, how his hand felt when I shook him and it didn't shake back.

Milo clears his throat, still standing in the doorway, one eyebrow raised. "What was that about?"

"I got a callback," I say, my voice flat, distant, like the words aren't mine.

"For what?"

I look at him like he's dumb, and he's still got that faintly bored look on his face, like the idea of me being important enough to get a phone call is something he can't quite believe. "For the movie I've been talking about for weeks," I say simply, and his expression flickers, just slightly, just enough for me to feel it in my chest.

"Congrats," he says, but it sounds hollow, like he's already forgotten what we're talking about. He turns and disappears down the hall, leaving me sitting on the futon, still holding the phone, still clutching the receipt like it might disappear if I let go.

The room is quiet now, the only sound the faint buzz of the TV, some infomercial for a miracle cleaning product playing in the background. My chest feels tight, my hands shaking just enough to notice. I think about Lars again, about the way the paramedics zipped him into that bag, about how Danielle hugged me so hard I thought she might squeeze me out of my skin.

I stare at the receipt, at the time and date scribbled in the corner, and for the first time in what feels like forever, I feel something sharp, something electric. Something alive.

Nine

My phone rings in the afternoon, loud and shrill and for a second, I think it's the casting director again, maybe calling to tell me the callback was a mistake, that they didn't mean to give me another shot. I roll over and grab my cell, the screen glowing with a number I know too well.

It's Ricky. Of course, it's Ricky.

I answer because part of me likes to let him talk, likes to see how far he'll go before I can't take it anymore. His voice is soft and stupid, his breathing shallow like he's rehearsed this. "I've been thinking about you," he says, his words curling through the phone like cigarette smoke. "I miss you. I still love you."

The laughter comes out of me before I can stop it, sharp and ugly, the kind of laugh that cuts your throat on the way up. "You don't love me," I say, my voice flat, biting. "You love having something to hang yourself on."

He starts to say something else—some bullshit about how he's changed, how he's different now—but I hang up before he can finish. I don't need to hear it. The last time we saw each other I told him he was an asshole and I was leaving and moving to Los Angeles, and then he proved my point by sleeping with Samantha Arnold knowing I didn't like her, the following week. I still remember the sting of her message.

Hey bitch. Just fucked your ex-boyfriend. XO

I toss the phone onto the mattress and stare at the ceiling, my pulse vibrating in my ears. Part of me wants to call him back, not to say anything, but just to hear him squirm. To let him know he's still just a ghost of a person, still sitting in his car somewhere in small town Illinois, choking on his own desperation.

I'm still thinking about it when the phone rings again, another number I don't recognize. I hesitate for a second, my thumb hovering over the screen, but something in me itches to pick up, like it's the universe calling and I might miss it.

"Hello?"

"Hi, is this Alexa Valentine?" The voice is crisp, feminine, the kind of voice that's used to getting what it wants. "This is Julia Harris, I'm a reporter with *The LA Times*. I was hoping to speak with you about Lars Bauer."

I blink, sitting up slowly, the room tilting slightly as the blood rushes to my head. "What about him?" I say, my voice guarded, though I already know where this is going.

"We're doing a piece about his passing," she says. "He was such a unique talent, and of course, his death has been such a tragedy for the community. We'd love to include a perspective from someone who was close to him. Would you be open to an interview?"

I let her talk, her voice pouring through the phone like syrup, sticky and sweet. She calls him "handsome," "charismatic," says he was "loved by everyone who knew him." Lars, the man who made a career out of dying in B-movies, who smoked too much and talked too loud and never once stopped to think about the mess he left behind. His official cause of death is a drug overdose, but she says it like its poetry, like he was *lost* to it, not swallowed whole.

"Sure," I say finally, surprising myself. "I'll do it."
There's a pause, just long enough to feel like she's sizing me up through the phone. "That's great," she says, and then, as if it's casual, like she's offering advice, she adds, "Just come as you are. Don't wear any makeup, don't get too dressed up. We want it to feel raw, authentic."

I don't laugh this time, but I want to. I want to shove the phone into my mouth and scream until it cracks. Instead, I press the receiver closer to my ear and say, "Fuck you. I'm wearing whatever I want."

She tries to backtrack, stumbling over herself, but I'm already smiling, sharp and bright, the kind of smile that makes people nervous. "I'll do your little interview," I say, "but I'm showing up in full makeup. Eyeliner. Lipstick. The works. And you know what? You're going to love it. Because there's nothing you can do about it."

She's quiet for a second, and I imagine her sitting at her desk, her perfectly manicured fingers hovering over her keyboard, trying to figure out how to spin this. "Of course," she says finally, her voice stiff, clipped. "Whatever makes you comfortable."

I don't know what got into me in that moment but I hang up without saying goodbye, the smile still tugging at the corners of my mouth. I get up and walk to the mirror, staring at my reflection, my face pale and puffy, my hair a mess. I don't care. I'm going to smear on red lipstick, line my eyes like warpaint, and sit in front of that reporter like I own the room.

Because Lars is dead, Ricky is a joke, and the only thing I know how to do is make them watch me.

Ten

The morning smells like burnt coffee and car exhaust, the air thick with heat and the slow rot of the city. I stop at Dunkin' Donuts because my stomach feels hollow, and I haven't eaten anything in two days except for half of a Pop-Tart I found in the bottom of my purse. Inside, it's colder than it has any right to be, the AC turned up so high I feel it settle on my skin like a second layer. I walk to the counter, my heels clicking against the sticky tile, and order an iced coffee, black, no sugar, because I don't trust myself not to drink the entire thing.

As I wait, I feel him looking at me. The man in the corner, wearing a white baseball cap that's too bright and a windbreaker that makes him look like he's about to sell me insurance. At first, it's the regular look—the up and down, the quick flick of his eyes that says he's cataloging me, my skirt, my legs, the curve of my back. I ignore it. Men like him are wallpaper, always there, always leering, always thinking they have a right to the space I take up.

But then he does a double take, his neck snapping like he's trying to make sure it's really me. "Hey," he says, his voice too loud for the quiet of the store. "You're that chick, right?"
I turn to him slowly, deliberately, my face blank. "What?"

"You're the one from the news," he says, grinning now, like we've met before, like we're friends. "You were dating that guy who overdosed. Lars something." He snaps his fingers. "Yeah, I saw. Crazy, man. That's crazy."

For a second, I just stare at him, my brain empty, my body still. Then I shake my head, short and sharp, like I'm shaking him off me, like I can make him disappear just by refusing to acknowledge him. I turn back to the counter, grab my coffee, and walk out, my heels catching on the edge of the door as I stumble into the street.

The sun is too bright, the world too loud, the iced coffee already sweating in my hand. I stand there for a second, the Dunkin' Donuts sign buzzing faintly behind me, and I feel like I might scream. Or cry. Or throw the coffee into the gutter just to watch it spill. But I don't do any of those things. I suck down half of it in one go, the bitterness jolting me awake, and start walking toward the studio for the second callback for *Lovers in the Dusk*. I'm so close I can taste it.

When I get there, the building is exactly what I expected: beige and forgettable, tucked between a dry cleaner and a payday loan place. Inside, the receptionist doesn't look up as I walk in, her nails clicking against the keyboard, her hair pulled back so tight it looks painful. I stand at the desk for a moment, waiting for her to notice me, before I clear my throat loudly.

She glances up, her eyes flicking over me in a way that feels surgical, and then back down at her screen. "Name?"

"Alexa Valentine," I say confidently, the name rolling off my tongue.

She types something into the computer, her nails clicking faster now, and then gestures toward the hallway without looking at me. "Second door on the left."

This callback I don't have to wait in a room with a bunch of girls who think they're better than me, I immediately get to go in and audition. I've leveled up.

I walk past the receptionist without saying thank you, my heels loud on the polished floor, my iced coffee still clutched in my hand. The studio is small, the kind of room that feels too small no matter how many people are in it. The same casting director from last time is sitting at a table with two different people, all of them wearing the same unreadable expressions, their pens poised over clipboards like they're ready to write me off before I even open my mouth.

"Alexa," the director says, her tone clipped, polite but distant. She gestures toward the center of the room, the light hitting her glasses in a way that makes her look like she's staring through me. "Whenever you're ready."

I set the coffee down on the floor, taking my time, my movements deliberate. I smooth my skirt, tuck my hair behind my ear, and step into the light, letting it fall over me like it's supposed to be there. I don't rush. I don't apologize. I stand there, tall and steady, and let them wait.

When I start, my voice is low, quiet, the kind of voice that makes people lean in, that makes them listen. The lines feel like mine now, like they've been living in my throat, waiting for this moment. I hold the pauses just a little too long, let the silence stretch like a held breath, and when I finish, I don't move. I let the air settle around me, heavy and electric, and then I step back, my heels clicking once against the floor.

The casting director looks at me for a moment, her pen hovering over the clipboard, and I can't tell if she's impressed or just calculating. "Thank you," she says finally, her tone even, neutral. "We'll be in touch."

I pick up my coffee, still cold, still bitter, and walk out without looking back. The receptionist doesn't even glance at me as I leave, but I don't care. Outside, the sun is still too bright, the world still too loud, but for the first time all day, I feel steady. I feel like I've taken up space and left a mark, like I'm something that won't disappear the second the door closes behind me.

Eleven

The next month moves fast, like the city itself has been sped up. Everything is blurring and loud, the noise constant, the lights brighter than they've ever been. The interview with the news station airs on a Tuesday night. I watch it at Danielle's insistence, sitting on the futon with her knee pressed into mine. She's holding a glass of wine and whispering, *you look incredible,* and I know she's right because I made sure of it.

I'd gone full production for the shoot, makeup sharp and glistening, a baby pink halter top that clung to my body in a way that said *I'm fragile but expensive.* I leaned into every question with just enough hesitation to feel real. When they asked me about Lars, I let my face crumple, a controlled demolition. I cried at all the right times, bit my lip when I needed to look brave, tilted my head just enough to catch the light. I said things like, *he was my person* and *I'll never love anyone like that again,* and they ate it up, the camera zooming in on my wet eyelashes, the curve of my mouth trembling like it was a performance even I didn't believe was fake.

It worked. The clip of me crying made its way online within hours, and from there, it was wildfire. People called me "hot crying girl." There were photos of my face, tear-streaked and luminous, captioned with things like *when he breaks your heart but you're still the hottest bitch alive.* There were memes. Fan pages. Gossip blogs where people analyzed the way I tilted my chin, the exact shade of lipstick I wore, the way my grief looked like art.

It was stupid. But it worked.

Two weeks later, a third callback for *Lovers in Dusk* came through. I showed up in ripped jeans and a white bedazzled tank top, no makeup, my hair loose and careless, like I'd rolled out of bed and still looked better than everyone else in the room. I walked in like I belonged there, and when I left, I already knew. The call came that night. I got the part. The lead. The girl whose face would be on the poster, whose name would be whispered in theaters.

There were whispers, of course. That I only got it because of Lars, because of the viral clip on the news, because the internet had turned me into something profitable. I knew what people were saying, but I didn't care. I'd won. It didn't matter how or why.

By the end of the month, everything had changed. I quit the gas station on a Tuesday afternoon, pulling off my name tag and tossing it onto the counter like it was the only thing tethering me to that version of myself. I walked out in the middle of my shift and now I smelled like Viva La Juicy all day and not gasoline for the first time in a year. It felt good. It felt great.

I signed with an agent. Not just any agent, but *the* agent, a woman named Lisa who looked like she'd been carved out of marble, a woman of fifty with a smooth botoxed face, her black hair cut into a blunt bob that made her look untouchable. She told me I was a star, said it like it was a fact, like I'd always been one and just didn't know it yet. Which I already knew, but it was nice to hear someone else say it for once. She told me she was going to make me *huge,* and I believed her. I had to.

There were talks about a TV show, something indie and dramatic, the kind of show where women cry in silk robes and throw wine in each other's faces. I was in meetings, fittings, shoots. I was everywhere. My MySpace exploded, my inbox flooded with strangers telling me I was beautiful, that they wanted to be me, that I was going to change everything.

It all started when Lars died. I think about that sometimes, late at night, when the noise quiets down and I'm left with just the memory of his face slack against the pillow, his skin pale and damp. I think about how none of this would've happened if he'd lived, if I hadn't cried just right for the camera, if people hadn't decided my grief was a commodity worth investing in.

My life feels like a music video on loop. Glossy, chaotic, full of light and noise. I don't care if it's fake. I don't care if it's built on nothing. What matters is that I'm here, that I'm seen, that people are looking.

Twelve

The parties start to come quickly, one after another, like someone turned a faucet on and forgot to shut it off. I bring Danielle because she fits into this world better than I do—thin and sharp and mean in a way that reads as confidence. She has the kind of face people stare at; the kind of laugh that makes them come closer. She drinks everything anyone puts in her hand, and it never shows on her. I watch her sometimes, the way she moves through a room like it's hers, her heels clicking on marble, her eyes scanning for someone worth remembering.

We go to these parties because it's what you're supposed to do, and because someone told me once that all the real decisions in Hollywood happen in kitchens at 2 a.m., over someone else's expensive tequila. The houses are always the same: big and glassy, perched on hills that feel dangerous in heels, the smell of chlorine bleeding in from the infinity pools. There are always the same kinds of people—men who look like they were born wearing blazers, women with wet, shiny faces who don't blink enough. They hand me drinks and talk too fast, their eyes darting to Danielle, then back to me, like they're trying to decide which of us is worth more.

At one of these parties, I meet Sam. He's leaning against a bookshelf like it owes him money, a half-full drink in his hand, his shirt unbuttoned just enough to show the edge of a tattoo. His platinum spiked hair is messy in that deliberate way, the kind that takes too long to look like you don't care, and he's not laughing at anyone's jokes. His eyes catch mine as I walk past, and he does this thing where he raises one eyebrow, just barely, like he's daring me to come over.

Danielle nudges me, her glass already empty. "He's hot," she says, her voice low, bored. "But he looks like he'll ruin your life."

I don't say anything. I just walk over, letting my heels click against the hardwood, the sound sharp and deliberate, like an invitation.

"You're the crying girl," he says, before I can even introduce myself.

I blink at him, caught off guard. "Yeah. What about it?"

He smirks, taking a sip of his drink. "I've seen your face all over the internet. You cry pretty."

The way he says it makes me want to hit him and kiss him at the same time, which is probably the point. I tilt my head, pretending to be amused, pretending to be the version of myself that belongs here. "Glad you liked the show."

"I didn't say I enjoyed it," he says, his voice flat, and then he grins like he can see right through me.

We talk for a while, though I don't remember what about. He says something about the parties being all the same, something about how everyone here is lying about something, including me. I tell him he's full of shit, but he's pretty enough that I don't leave.

Later, much later, after Danielle is finally drunk enough to be distracted by some older man with a bad tan and I'm tired of the way everyone keeps looking at me like I'm something they can use, Sam finds me on the patio. He's got his keys in his hand, dangling them lazily, like he knows I'll follow. "Let's go for a drive," he says, not even waiting for me to agree.

His car is parked down the street, a sleek black Porsche that smells like leather and money. The seats are low, almost too low, and the air inside is cool, silent, like the whole world has disappeared. He doesn't talk as he drives, his hand loose on the wheel, his eyes flicking to me every so often like he's waiting for me to break the silence.

We stop at a red light, and he turns to me, his face unreadable. "Do you want me to kiss you?" he asks, like it's a challenge, like he already knows the answer.

I don't say yes, but I don't say no either, and that's enough. His mouth is rough, insistent, and when he pulls back, his eyes are darker than before. He reaches over, his hand sliding up my thigh, pulling up my hot pink latex skirt, his fingers warm against my skin, and I don't stop him.

He leans down without saying anything, his body folding awkwardly in the small space, his head disappearing below the steering wheel, pulling my panties down around my ankles. I stare out the window, the world outside blurry and dark, the city humming softly around us. His mouth is warm and precise,

47

and I sink back into the seat, my fingers gripping the leather, my head tilted just enough to feel the sharp edge of the window against my temple.

When it's over, he sits up, his face flushed, his grin lazy. "You taste expensive," he says, like it's a joke, but there's something about the way he looks at me that makes my chest feel tight.

"Don't get used to it," I say, my voice sharper than I mean it to be. "Now let's go back to the party. My friend is probably wondering where I am."

He laughs, low and quiet like I said something funny, and starts the car without another word. The engine purrs, and we pull back into the night, the city spreading out in front of us like it's ours for the taking.

Thirteen

The photo is everywhere. Grainy and dark, but clear enough to make out my face pressed against the window, my mouth slightly open, Josh Gracin's body bent between my knees, folded into the sharp angles of his Porsche. My first thought is how ugly it looks, not sexy at all, nothing like the magazines, just limbs and heat and desperation. My second thought is, *who the fuck is Josh Gracin?*

I'm scrolling through my phone at the kitchen table, the sunlight slanting through the blinds in harsh, uneven stripes. My coffee is cold, and Danielle is sitting across from me, her spoon clinking softly against the sides of her cereal bowl. Milo is already hunched over his laptop, looking up this Josh Gracin, clicking too loud, scrolling too fast. I can feel their attention pivot toward me, sharp and curious, their movements slowing as the search results load.

His mugshot fills the screen first—sharper jawline than I remember, his hair messy in that calculated way that fooled me into thinking he was something else. Below the photo, the words punch through the silence: *Oil Tycoon Arrested for DUI That Killed One Woman and Her Dog.*

I close my phone without saying anything, shove my chair back hard enough to scrape the tile. The sound echoes in the kitchen, but no one stops me. Danielle watches me go, her spoon still hovering mid-air, her mouth pressed into a thin, curious line, already filing this away for later.

The next day, the call comes early. My agent Lisa. I can tell by her voice that this isn't good news. It's flat, deliberate, the cadence of someone who's been rehearsing the same bad lines for years. She tells me about the photo, about the blogs, about the people on MySpace tearing me apart, about the word *optics,* and what it means for someone like me, someone who cried pretty enough to go viral but not enough to make mistakes.

The sitcom offer is gone. It doesn't matter that it wasn't my fault, that I didn't know his real name, that I didn't know someone was crouched in the shadows with a camera. What matters is how it looks. And it looks bad. She says the words carefully, slowly, like she thinks I might shatter. Like I haven't been here before.

I sit there on the edge of my futon, her voice buzzing in my ear, too crisp against the silence of the room. Lars' face flashes in my mind, pale and slack, the shape of him still imprinted on my sheets. This all started with him, with the way I cried for the cameras, with the way the internet decided my grief was just pretty enough to turn into currency. I rub the back of my hand against my eyes, but it's too dry for tears.

She tells me there's a way out. A way to fix it. She says it like it's a favor, like it's a gift. She says she has a client, a good guy, someone who looks like stability, like structure, like a moral reboot. She says the public loves a redemption story, that if I date him, just for a little while, the narrative will shift. People will forget about the photo, about Josh Gracin. They'll see me as someone worth saving again.

I sit there, the phone pressed against my ear, the cold air from the window crawling across my skin. She tells me his name, but I don't hear it. My eyes are fixed on the corner of the room, where Lars used to lean, where his jacket still hangs limp on the back of the chair. I think about the way I cried on TV, the way I made them look, the way I told them a story they wanted to believe. I think about the sitcom, the Porsche, the quiet click of the camera, and the sound of my name slipping out of their mouths like a curse.

I don't say yes. I don't say no. I just sit there, letting the silence stretch, my agent's voice humming softly in the distance, too far away to touch.

Fourteen

I buy a gun from Two-Time Johnny, this Italian guy who owns the laundromat around the corner. He has the look of someone who should have mob ties but doesn't, not anymore, probably because he fucked something up and now spends his days fixing washing machines. He doesn't ask why I need it, and I don't offer an explanation. We go into his office. He leans back in his chair while I hand him the money, chewing on a toothpick, his other hand resting on the shotgun like it's a family heirloom.

"Good choice," he says, sliding it across the counter like we're closing on a used car.

I take it and head home, stopping for lunch which is just an iced coffee on the way. When I get back, I sit on the floor of my room and look up a few videos on how to load it, how to aim, how to not blow my own face off in the process. It's easier than I thought, the clicks and snaps of the shells sliding into place weirdly satisfying. I watch a few more videos while the gun sits across my lap, cold and heavier than I expected. I could get used to the weight.

My phone buzzes. I glance at it, already knowing who it is. My fake boyfriend, Hallmark movie actor Kurt Monaghan. The actor my agent saddled me with to make me look wholesome again. He's a nice guy, objectively attractive, but every time he texts me, it feels like my soul is getting sanded down by a nail file. He writes, *Can't wait to see you tomorrow night. Thinking about you,* and I roll my eyes so hard it hurts. We have been hanging out for three weeks and I still haven't let him fuck me yet. He knows it's a PR relationship, but he still acts like we're a real couple.

Even Josh Gracin, DUI murderer, had more charisma. At least he left bite marks.

I toss the phone onto my bed and check the time. Almost 4. I load the gun, the shells sliding in smooth and easy, and wait.

Dave comes home first, right on time, walking through the door with that same dumb expression he always has, like he's surprised to find himself here. He drops his bag by the door, muttering something about work, pulling off his jacket without even looking at me. I stand up, grab the shotgun from behind the couch, and walk right up to him.

When he finally turns, his eyes flick down to the gun, then back to my face. He doesn't even get a word out before I pull the trigger. The blast knocks me back a step, my ears ringing, but it doesn't hurt. Dave, though—Dave goes down immediately, his head splitting open like a fruit dropped from a great height. Blood and brain matter splash the walls, the floor, the couch. A chunk of his skull lands on the coffee table, and I take a moment to pick it up and toss it onto the rug.

The mess is worse than I expected. I reload the gun, the motions smooth now, almost instinctive, and wait for Milo to get home.

He comes in about an hour later, jingling his keys like it's a normal day, like he isn't about to lose it all in the doorway. I shoot him before he even gets his shoes off, the blast ripping through his chest, sending him crumpling against the kitchen counter. His body slides down, leaving a streak of blood on the cabinets, his mouth still half-open like he was about to tell me about some conspiracy theory he'd read on the internet.

When it's over, I set the gun down and start cleaning up. Not the blood—I'm not a miracle worker—but the details. I strip them both down to their boxers, dragging their bodies into the living room and laying them side by side. Dave is heavier than I thought, and Milo's dead weight makes my arms ache, but I don't stop until they're lying neat and symmetrical, like two dolls left behind by a careless child.

I step back to look at them, brushing a strand of hair out of my face. They look almost peaceful, like they could've done this to each other if I wasn't here. I change my clothes and then I sit on the couch and call the cops.

When they arrive, the house fills with the sound of boots on the floor, radios crackling, voices murmuring just loud enough for me to catch words like *messy* and *gruesome*. One of the officers looks down at the bodies, his face blank, and mutters, *Classic lovers' quarrel. Murder-suicide.*

I almost laugh. Instead, I lean back against the couch and pretend to cry, letting the noise of the scene wash over me. No one asks me too many questions, their eyes flicking to the gun, to the blood, to the carefully arranged bodies like they already know the story. And I let them believe it, because it's easier than the truth, because the truth doesn't matter. I wait for them to leave, the quiet pressing back into the room, and wonder if Two-Time Johnny has something smaller I can carry in my purse.

Fifteen

Me and my fake boyfriend go to a romantic dinner because it's what couples do. Kurt picked the place, and it's exactly the kind of spot I expected—low lighting, high prices, the kind of vibe that makes you feel important. The host seats us by the window, naturally, and I feel the weight of the cameras outside, the flashbulbs cutting through the dark like lightning.

Kurt sits across from me, his blazer too big at the shoulders, his hair stiff with gel that smells faintly of lemons. He's got this T-shirt on under the blazer that says something ironic that I can't fully read—probably a line from a sitcom nobody remembers—and I can already tell he's spent all day rehearsing how to make this look effortless and it takes everything in me not to scream *you're a fucking nerd* at maximum volume.

He fumbles with the menu like it's written in another language. I sit back and watch him squint at the options, his lips moving as he tries to sound it out.

"What are you getting?" he asks, finally looking up, his voice soft like we're sharing something intimate.

"I don't know," I say, flipping the menu shut. "Maybe the arsenic."

He blinks, his expression wobbling somewhere between confusion and unease. "What?"

"The arsenic," I repeat, my voice flat. "I hear it pairs well with a dry white."

He laughs, but it's thin, and I can see his brain trying to decide if this is a joke. I hold his gaze a second too long, then glance out the window where the paparazzi are already shooting like we're the cover story.

He orders the duck, mangling the pronunciation so badly the waiter has to repeat it with a polite, almost pitying smile. I order a salad that costs the same as a pair of jeans, and the waiter nods like we've made some excellent choices.

Kurt talks while we wait, his words spilling out in awkward bursts, mostly about himself. He tells me about some indie project he passed on because the director didn't "get his vibe," and I watch him fold and refold his napkin like he's trying to build a tiny paper monument to his own mediocrity.

"You ever eat a person?" I ask, cutting him off mid-sentence.

His head jerks up, his mouth half-open. "What?"

"Human flesh," I say, leaning forward slightly. "I hear it tastes like pork. You ever try it?"

He stares at me like I just started speaking in tongues. "No," he says finally, his voice cracking.

"You should," I say, leaning back again. "It's really enlightening."

The food arrives before he can respond, and it's just as disappointing as I thought it'd be. His duck looks like a tiny, overworked corpse, and my salad is limp and bitter, a handful of greens pretending to be worth forty dollars. We eat in silence, Kurt occasionally glancing at me like he's trying to figure out if I'm insane or just mean.

After dinner, we go to a movie because that's what normal couples do, and we're supposed to look normal. Kurt picks some action flick, the kind where the plot doesn't matter as long as things explode in slow motion. The theater is almost empty, the air thick with the smell of popcorn that's been sitting under a heat lamp for too long.

We sit in the back, and Kurt spends the first fifteen minutes whispering about the symbolism of car chases like I didn't already know he's full of shit. His voice is loud enough to earn a glare from the couple in front of us, and I sink lower in my seat, pretending I don't know him.

Halfway through, he tries to touch my leg. His hand hovers first, hesitant, his palm hovering like he's afraid my knee might bite him. When he finally rests it on my leg, it's damp and awkward, like he's trying to pet a wild animal.

"Don't," I say, not even looking at him.

He pulls back immediately, mumbling something about *mixed signals,* but I've already tuned him out.

After the movie, we walk back to his car, the night warm and sticky even though it's September. He fumbles with his keys, glancing at me like he's waiting for permission to speak.

"I think we're done," I say, sliding into the passenger seat.

"Done with what?" he asks, his voice soft and unsure, like he's afraid of the answer.

"This," I say, gesturing between us. "The fake dates. The pretending. I'm not really good at it."

He stares at me, his mouth opening and closing like he's rehearsing a rebuttal, but nothing comes out. "But Lisa said—" he starts, but I cut him off.

"Lisa doesn't have to sit through your bad jokes," I say, adjusting my seatbelt. "You'll survive."

When we get to my place, I hop out of his car without saying goodbye. As I walk away, I flip open my cell phone and scroll through the grainy photos already online—Kurt and me laughing over dinner, walking into the theater, his hand grazing my back.

I'll call Lisa tomorrow and explain, she'll understand. By tomorrow, they'll say I broke his heart. He'll get a pity piece in some blog or magazine, and I'll be the bitch who broke his heart but at least they'll be talking about me.

Sixteen

The set smells like burnt coffee and hairspray, the air thick with the sound of people moving without looking, their heads down, their voices clipped and too fast. I'm starring opposite Tess Baker in some made-for-TV drama about betrayal and friendship or whatever, though the friendship part feels like a stretch.

She's supposed to be my best friend in the movie, but every time the camera isn't rolling, she acts like being near me is a punishment she doesn't deserve.   I'm still blackballed by half of Hollywood because of what happened with Josh Gracin. My agent says I'm lucky. I'm *popular,* and that's still worth something. People don't have to like me—they just have to keep saying my name. Plus, the murder-suicide of my roommates really gave me sympathy points. Luckily, my faux breakup with Kurt Monaghan didn't make waves like we thought it would. My agent kept track, combing the gossip blogs obsessively. I was in the clear on that one. Apparently Kurt Monaghan was not as liked as Lisa thought. Now I'm here, taking what I can get, pretending not to notice the way everyone on set looks at me like I'm radioactive. We're shooting a scene where Tess's character is supposed to comfort mine after my husband leaves me, but the director keeps stopping us, shouting notes to Tess about tone and connection, like she's not giving enough. And she's not. She barely looks at me, her body stiff and coiled, like she's allergic to my presence. Between takes, she stares at her phone, her jaw tight, her hand gripping the back of her chair like she's ready to bolt.

After we finish the scene, the director calls for a break, and I watch Tess march toward her trailer without a word. I sit in my chair for a minute, sipping lukewarm water from a plastic bottle, my stomach tight with something between anger and boredom. Then I stand up and follow her.

Her trailer is small and stuffy, the air inside heavy with the smell of floral body spray and whatever overpriced skincare product she's slathered all over her face. She's sitting on the couch, scrolling through her phone, her lips pressed into a hard line. When she looks up and sees me, her expression sharpens, like she's been waiting for this.

"Can I help you?" she asks, her tone brittle, sharp.

"Yeah," I say, stepping inside and closing the door behind me. "What's your problem with me?"

She puts her silver Motorola Razr down slowly, deliberately, like she's deciding how much effort I'm worth. "You really don't know?"

"No," I say, crossing my arms. "Enlighten me."

She sighs, like this is exhausting for her, like I'm exhausting for her. "There's a rumor going around that you said something about me. Something nasty."

I blink at her, my head tilting slightly. "What?"

"I don't know. Something about how I'm hard to work with, how I'm a diva—"

"I hate to say it," I cut in, my voice flat, "but you're not important enough for me to spread rumors about."

The words land like a slap, her face hardening immediately, her cheeks flushing with anger. She stands up, her body tense, her hands clenched at her sides. "You're unbelievable," she says, her voice rising. "You walk around like you're untouchable, like you're some kind of star, but you're a fucking *joke.* You're a tabloid headline. You're—"

"Shut up," I snap, stepping closer to her. "You don't know anything about me."

She doesn't back down. "I know enough. I know you'll do anything to stay relevant, even if it means destroying everyone around you."

The fight happens fast, faster than I can think. She steps toward me, her hand flying up like she's about to point, to jab her finger in my face, but I react without thinking, grabbing her wrist and shoving her backward. She stumbles, her heel catching on the edge of the carpet, and she falls hard, her head cracking against the corner of the table.

For a moment, everything is still. Her body slumps to the floor, her head at a strange angle, blood pooling under her temple, soaking into the carpet. I stare at her, my chest heaving, my hands shaking.

"Tess?" I say, my voice barely a whisper.

She doesn't move. Her face is pale, her eyes half-closed, her mouth slack.

I kneel down slowly, my knees pressing into the rough carpet, and reach out to touch her shoulder. There's no breath, no sound, no movement. My hand hovers over her face, trembling, and I realize—she's dead.

The blood spreads fast, dark and glistening, soaking into her pristine white blouse, into the floor, into everything. My stomach churns, but I can't move, can't breathe. My mind is blank, a white noise hum drowning out everything except the sight of her lifeless body.

I stand up finally, my legs unsteady, my chest tight. The room smells like iron, like sweat, like panic. I don't know what to do. I don't know how to fix this.

The door to the trailer feels impossibly far away, but I make it there, stepping over her body, the sound of my footsteps loud in the silence. I open the door and step outside, the sunlight blinding, the noise of the set crashing into me like a wave.

I close the door behind me and walk away, my face blank, my hands shaking. No one notices. No one stops me. They're all too busy, too distracted, too wrapped up in their own little dramas to notice that Tess isn't coming back. They'll figure it out soon.

Seventeen

My mom and sister come to visit me from Illinois for a week, their suitcases dragging behind them like dead animals. I pick them up from LAX in my rented cherry red Porsche, which I drove in circles before coming to the airport because I noticed paparazzi in a black car following me. Ever since Tess Baker was found dead in her trailer they've been following me even more now. I should love it. And apart of me does. I love the fame, even if it means it's because I'm the girl who is surrounded by death.

My mom looks out the window with her mouth pressed into a hard line, her hands folded in her lap like she's bracing for turbulence. My sister Cassandra sits in the back, silent except for the occasional sigh, her hair tied back too tight, her nails bitten down to the skin. She is two years younger than me at nineteen and still acts like a child with an anger problem. I also have an anger problem, but mine is more inward, whereas she wears hers like a neon suit.

They don't ask about the car, but I see it in their faces, the way my mom grips the seatbelt and my sister stares at the leather interior like it might swallow her whole. My mom talks about the flight, about how the man next to her smelled like onions, about how my sister got into a fight with the flight attendant because she didn't want to put her bag under the seat. My sister doesn't deny it. She just says, "The seats were fucking small," and picks at the hem of her sweatshirt.

When we get to my newly rented apartment, my mom stops just inside the door, looking around like she's trying to figure out if this is a real place or a set. The windows are too clean, the furniture too sharp, the air too still. After what happened with Dave and Milo, Danielle's dad put the house on the market and she moved to an apartment in Beverly Hills. I settled for an apartment in West Hollywood. It's not glamorous but it's quiet and has an extra large closet. I have a real bed now. I think about the futon bed sometimes, it made me feel like I survived something. Now I'm basking.

She sets her suitcase down slowly, carefully, and says, "This is nice," but her voice is tight, like she doesn't believe it. My sister doesn't say anything. She drops her bag on the floor, flops onto the couch, and pulls out her phone.

I offer them drinks, coffee, water, wine, but my mom just shakes her head, and my sister doesn't look up. I pour myself a glass of tequila and sprite and sit down across from them, my legs crossed, my smile too wide.

"How's work?" my mom asks finally, her hands still folded in her lap.

"It's good," I say, my voice light, easy. "Busy. I just finished shooting a movie. Something small, but it's getting a lot of buzz."

"That's great," she says, but the words feel flat, like she's trying to read a script she doesn't understand.

My sister snorts, still staring at her phone. "You're in some drama again, aren't you?" she says. "There was some article about you on Perez last week. Something about...what was it? A fight? Or someone dying?"

My mom shoots her a look, sharp and quick, and my sister rolls her eyes but doesn't say anything else.

"It's just rumors," I say, my voice steady, practiced. "You know how the press is. They'll say anything for clicks. Tess Baker had an accident and died in her trailer. Had nothing to do with me."

"That's terrible."

I take a swig of my drink. "Yeah. Tragic. They replaced her with this Canadian actress named Heather Welch. I liked her way more than Tess and we had good chemistry. So, it all worked out in the end."

My mom nods, but I can see it in her face—the doubt, the worry, the way she's trying not to ask the questions she really wants to ask. My sister doesn't care. She's already moved on, her thumbs flying over the screen, her face lit up in the glow of her phone.

That first night we order Chinese takeout for dinner because I don't cook, and my mom spends the whole meal asking me questions about the apartment, the neighborhood, the people I work with, but never about me, and how I'm doing. My sister barely eats, picking at her food, her eyes keep darting up from her plate to me like she's trying to figure out who I've turned into.

I take them on a tour across LA and we go shopping and eat good food and talk but nothing really of importance. At night we watch movies on my giant flatscreen television, making snarky comments about an actor's appearance or making fun of the way they deliver their lines. Not many will understand but this is how my family bonds. We don't say *I love you*, we don't have deep talks, we just like to sit in each other's presence, and that was enough.

By the time they leave a week later, the apartment feels heavier, like they've left something behind. My mom hugs me at the door, her arms tight around me, and says, "Be careful," her voice low, her breath warm against my ear. My sister doesn't hug me. She just nods, her face unreadable, and follows my mom out the door without looking back. I watch them climb into their taxi and I stand there for a moment after they're gone, the silence settling over me like a second skin.

I pour another drink, sit on the couch, and stare at the city lights through the window, thinking about the way my mom looked at the apartment, the way my sister wouldn't meet my eyes, the way they still see me as the girl I left behind in Illinois, the girl I can't be anymore.

Eighteen

Two-Time Johnny leans against the counter at the laundromat, his gold chain catching the light like gold-digger bait. He always smells faintly of dryer sheets and weed, his toothpick moving lazily from one corner of his mouth to the other. His whole persona feels like a suit that doesn't fit—borrowed stories, borrowed danger, borrowed menace—but there's something in the way he looks at me today, slow and heavy, that makes my stomach twist just enough to notice.

"I need something smaller," I say, casual, like we're talking about detergent or quarters or the weather.

He doesn't answer right away, just lets the grin spread across his face, slow and deliberate. "Yeah, I can get you something," he says finally, his voice low and steady. "But there's a price."

I tilt my head, feigning curiosity, though I already know what's coming.

"You're gonna have to give me something first," he says, and the words land like the punchline to a bad joke. "And I'm not talking about money."

I blink at him, my face carefully blank, my body still.

"And if I don't?" I ask, my voice soft, bored, like this is a conversation I've already forgotten.

He shrugs, the movement lazy but calculated, like he's practiced it. "Then I'll have people come looking for you. People who won't be as nice as me."

It's bullshit. I know it's bullshit. Two-Time Johnny isn't in the mob—he's a guy who spent a year in county jail for putting some guy in a coma after a bar fight and came out thinking he could pass for a wise guy. I'd done my research, pieced together his life from half-legible mugshots and police reports. He's not dangerous. He's desperate. But desperation is messy, and I don't feel like making a scene here, in the laundromat with its buzzing lights and the detergent-stained walls.

So I take him back to my apartment.

We fuck fast and hard, his hands rough, his movements frantic, like he's trying to prove something to me, to himself, to some invisible person he thinks is watching. He keeps his chain on, the gold bouncing against his chest, catching the light in flashes. He finishes quickly, with a low grunt that sounds more like defeat than satisfaction, and I stare at the ceiling, waiting for him to roll off me. When he does, his body is damp and heavy, his breath loud and uneven, and he doesn't notice when I reach under the bed.

The metal bat feels solid in my hands, its weight grounding me, calming me. I grip it tightly, my fingers curling around the handle like I was born to hold it. He's sitting on the edge of the bed now, his back to me, his shoulders hunched as he pulls on his socks.

I stand up on the bed slowly, lift the bat over his head and swing.

The first hit lands with a sickening crack, right against the side of his head. His body folds instantly, collapsing onto the floor in a heap, his arms sprawled out like a child mid-tantrum. Blood sprays across the carpet, dark and wet, pooling around him in a slow, spreading circle. I swing again, harder this time, the impact vibrating through my arms, and his skull gives way with a sound like wet paper tearing.

The room smells like iron now, sharp and metallic, and the walls are streaked with red. His chain is still glinting faintly, the gold slick with blood, and for a moment, I can't look away from it.

I drop the bat, the sound of it hitting the floor louder than it should be, and sit down on the edge of the bed. My chest is heaving, my hands sticky and trembling, but my mind is quiet, clear.

Two-Time Johnny is dead. His head is a mess of bone and blood and brain, the carpet beneath him soaked through, the room painted with the proof of what I've done. And I feel nothing.

After a while, I grab a towel and wipe the bat clean, wrapping it tightly before sliding it back under the bed. The body is still warm, still leaking, and I know I should feel something—guilt, regret, panic—but all I feel is a faint hum in the back of my skull, a sense of calm settling over me like fog. The cleanup will take hours, but I've got time.

Nineteen

I chop up Two-Time Johnny in the bathtub. His flesh is tougher than I thought it would be, his tendons thick and resistant, like he's still trying to fight back. The sawblade slips in my hands, slick with blood, and I have to stop every few minutes to wipe it clean on a towel already soaked through. His bones are the loudest part, cracking like wet branches, the sound bouncing off the tile walls and making my ears ring.

The tub fills with pieces of him, pink and red and horribly wrong. The smell is overwhelming, copper and salt and something bitter, and it clings to my hair, my clothes, the inside of my mouth. When I'm done, I sit on the toilet, the saw still in my hand, and stare at what's left. His teeth are too neat, too bright, like they don't belong in this mess, so I grab the pliers from under the sink.

It takes longer than I expect. The roots are deep, stubborn, and each yank comes with a wet, sticky sound, a faint pop that makes my stomach lurch even as I pull harder. Blood seeps from his gums, pooling in the crevices of his mouth, staining my hands a deeper red. When I'm finished, I toss the teeth into the sink, where they clink against the porcelain, small and pale and strangely innocent.

I bag the pieces one by one, black trash bags lining up like soldiers at my feet. By the time I load them into the trunk, my arms ache, my legs tremble, but I don't stop. I can't.

The L.A. River is quieter than I expected. The smell of rot hangs in the air, faint but insistent, mingling with the sharp tang of industrial runoff. The riverbed is cracked and dry, the water a thin, sluggish trickle, but it's enough. I toss the bags in one by one, their shapes folding and sinking into the murk without a sound.

His chain hangs from the rearview mirror on the drive back, swinging gently with every turn, catching the moonlight like it's mocking me.

When I get home, the apartment smells like bleach and something sour, most likely bone fragments floating in the air. I shower, scrubbing at my hands, my arms, my thighs, but the smell won't leave, faint and metallic, lodged in the back of my throat like a memory.

I don't sleep. Instead, I lie in bed staring at the ceiling, the bat still tucked under the mattress, its weight a comfort I can't explain.

At 6 a.m., my alarm goes off. The commercial I'm doing today is for a deodorant, a low-stakes gig my agent practically begged me to take. "It's a paycheck," she said, "a chance to remind people you're still working." So I get up, pulling on something casual but expensive, and take the long way to the studio, driving past the river again.

The set is sterile, too clean. The kind of place that smells faintly of lemon cleaner and artificial calm. They sit me in a chair, slather my face with foundation, pull my hair into something neat and polished. I watch them work, their hands moving over me like I'm just another prop to be adjusted.

The script is short, just a few lines about confidence and freshness, but the words stick in my throat, heavy and cloying. Between takes, I sip from a bottle of water, the plastic cool and wet against my fingers.

The director claps after the final shot hours later, beaming like I just gave the performance of my life. The crew claps too, polite and distant, their eyes already moving past me. I smile, my lips tight, my teeth too sharp, and thank them before slipping out.

In the car, I stare at my reflection in the rearview mirror, at the faint streak of blood still caught under my nails, at the way my eyes look too dark, too wide. His chain sits heavy in my pocket, the metal warm against my skin, and I wonder if it'll ever feel light again.

At home, the bleach smell is still there, sharp and clean and failing to cover the rot beneath. I sit on the couch, the chain dangling from my fingers, and think about the teeth in the sink, the bags in the river, the corners of my mind that will never feel clean.

Twenty

Ricky calls me late, his voice crackling on the other end. I recognize his number immediately, even though I deleted it months ago. He doesn't say hello, just jumps in with, *I saw you on TV. You looked good.* I let the silence stretch, listening to the hum of his breathing on the other end of the line. I already know what he's going to say before he says it.

"I miss you," he murmurs, his voice low and warm, like we're still something we never were.

"Do you?" I ask, flat and bored twisting a piece of my hair around my finger.

"I'm coming to L.A.," he says, like it's a fact, like I should be thrilled. "I want to see you."

The pause between us feels like it's holding its breath. Then I say, "Okay."

We meet at a sleazy Mexican restaurant off Pico, the kind of place with cracked leather booths and fluorescent lights that make everyone look tired. The tacos are good—cheap and greasy, the kind that drip all over your hands before you can finish them. Ricky is already sitting at a corner table when I walk in, hunched over a michelada, his dark hair sticking up in greasy peaks, his face pale under the yellow glow.

He looks like someone I used to know, but not quite. He's softer around the edges now, heavier, his eyes rimmed with red like he's been crying or not sleeping or both. I slide into the booth across from him, and he looks up, his expression caught somewhere between nervous and hungry.

"You look good," he says again, his voice too loud in the quiet of the restaurant.

"Thanks," I say, picking up a menu I don't need.

We don't talk much. He orders nachos, and I get two tacos al pastor, which I eat slowly, the grease pooling in the paper wrapper, the meat soft and sweet. Ricky stares at me while he eats, his hands trembling slightly as he picks apart the edges of his chips, his eyes darting around like he's trying to memorize my face.

"I miss you," he says again, quieter this time, like he's embarrassed.

I set my taco down, leaning back against the booth. "Show me," I say, my voice low and even, daring him to move.

His mouth twitches like he wants to smile, but he doesn't. Instead, he just nods, his hand fumbling for his wallet as he throws cash on the table. I stand and walk out, not waiting for him, letting the air outside hit me like a slap, warm and sticky and too full of smog.

At my apartment, Ricky follows me inside like a dog on a leash, his hands shoved into his pockets, his shoulders hunched like he's bracing for something. I can feel the weight of him behind me, his breath quick and shallow, his eyes heavy on my back.

When we get to the living room, I turn to him, stepping close enough that I can smell the sourness of his sweat, the faint tang of michelada on his breath. I reach out, running a hand down his arm, and he shivers under my touch, his lips parting slightly.

"Take off your shirt," I say, and he does, fumbling with the buttons, his hands shaking so hard it takes longer than it should.

I don't tell him what to do next. I just pull him toward me, kissing him hard, my teeth scraping against his lip, tasting the salt of his skin. He groans, low and desperate, his hands gripping my waist like he thinks I might disappear.

Then I pull back, slowly, watching his face shift, his eyes wide and hazy, his lips swollen and wet. He doesn't notice when I reach for the knife on the counter, the blade cold and sharp in my hand.

I step behind him, my movements slow, deliberate, and slide the knife across his throat in one clean motion. The sound he makes is soft, almost surprised, like a gasp he can't quite finish. Blood spills out immediately, hot and dark, soaking into his shirt, splattering across the floor, the counter, my hands. He collapses onto his knees, his mouth opening and closing like he's trying to say something, but all that comes out is a wet, gurgling sound. "Why?" He whispers.

I watch him for a moment, my chest rising and falling, my hand still gripping the knife. "Because the man in my mouth told me to."

The blood pools around him, thick and glistening, the smell sharp and metallic, filling the air until it's all I can taste.

When it's over, I stand there for a while, staring down at his body, the way it folds in on itself, small and pathetic, his hands clutching at his throat like he can hold the life in. The knife is still warm in my hand, the blade slick and sticky, and I wipe it off on his shirt before setting it on the counter.

The apartment is quiet now, the only sound the faint hum of the fridge, the soft drip of blood hitting the tile. I grab a towel, start cleaning up, the motions automatic, mechanical. The blood comes off the floor easily, but the smell lingers, clinging to the air, to my skin, to the corners of my mind.

I toss his body into a tarp and the city hums outside my window, oblivious, endless. Somewhere, a car backfires, and I laugh to myself, soft and low, the sound bouncing off the walls like it doesn't belong to me.

Twenty-One

The next morning, my agent calls. Her voice slices through the stale air of my apartment, loud and sharp, too full of energy for this early. I snap my phone open and let her words wash over me.

"You've got an audition," she says, and I'm only half-listening until she drops his name: *Shane West.*

I sit up, my heart flipping like it used to when I saw my name in print for the first time. Shane West. America's heartthrob. Not A-list, but close enough. A name with just enough weight to pull me out of the muck I've been stuck in for months.

"You have to nail this Alexa," she says, like I don't already know. Like I don't spend every second figuring out how to keep my face on people's screens, how to keep them staring. "This is your shot."

She hangs up before I can even say anything. I snap the phone shut, lean back into my couch, and light a joint, the smoke curling around my face, filling my chest. The room smells faintly of blood, though I've scrubbed every inch of it, the bleach still stinging my nose. The plastic body parts are waiting for me, heavy and silent, but I don't move. Not yet.

After bingeing a few episodes of *The Real World*, I get up, finish cutting Ricky into smaller pieces, my hands steady, my breath even. The saw drags, catching on bone, but I've gotten used to the sound, the vibration running up my arms. When I'm done, I shove the pieces into the black trash bags and line them up by the door like guests who've overstayed their welcome.

I'm starving. I make a sandwich, eat it in four bites, but then I think about the tacos from last night, the grease on my fingers, the sweetness of the meat, and it makes my stomach twist. I go to the bathroom, kneel in front of the toilet, and press my fingers against the back of my throat. It comes up fast, sour and bitter, and I flush without looking.

By nightfall, I can't be in the apartment anymore. I dress quickly—tight baby pink bedazzled tank top and low-rise blue jeans, something that makes people look twice—and head to the club.

The place is packed, the music pounding, the lights strobing in colors that make everyone look flushed and unhinged. The air is thick with sweat and smoke and perfume, bodies pressed together like they're trying to forget themselves.

As soon as I walk in, people notice me. They always do. Someone whispers my name, loud enough for me to hear, and then there's a hand on my arm, a face too close to mine, a voice saying, *"Oh my God, are you…?"*

I smile, sharp and small, and let them buy me a drink. Vodka, straight. It burns going down, but I don't care. Another person joins us, then another, until I'm surrounded, the drinks piling up, hands brushing against my waist, my hair, my shoulders.

A guy offers me coke and I take it, the sharp rush making the lights feel brighter, the music louder. The guy who handed me the bag is talking too fast, his words slurring together, his eyes darting to my lips, my collarbone, the curve of my hips. I let him talk, nodding occasionally, my fingers trailing along the edge of his Ed Hardy shirt. I might take home with me.

I whisper in his ear to stay where he is while I go use the bathroom and even though he gives me a thumbs up in response when I come out, the guy is gone and the crowd feels closer, heavier, the air pressing against me like it knows something I don't, a girl grabs my hand, pulls me onto the dance floor, her nails digging into my wrist, her laughter ringing in my ears. I don't know who she is, but she keeps saying my name, her voice rising above the music,

Alexa Valentine, Alexa Valentine. Alexa Valentine. You are one hot bitch.

I let her pull me into a mass of bodies. We even make out for a bit. People are watching. They always are. Their eyes linger too long, their mouths curling into knowing smiles, their phones flashing like I'm something they need to capture, something they can hold onto for later.

Some rando hands me another drink, and I take it without thinking, the liquid warm and sweet and sticky. A guy with slicked-back hair leans in close, his hand resting on my lower back, his breath hot against my ear as he says, "You're trouble, aren't you?"

I laugh, loud and sharp, and pull away, disappearing into the crowd before he can follow. He wasn't even worth two seconds of my time.

By the time I leave, my head is buzzing, my body vibrating with the rhythm of the music, the lights still flashing in the corners of my vision. I stumble into a cab, ignoring the paparazzi flashing my photo, the bags of Ricky still waiting for me at home, the L.A. river calling like a promise.

When I get back, I finish the job quickly, the movements automatic now, like muscle memory. I'm still pretty drunk but I drive to the L.A. River, the city quiet and sprawling around me, and toss the pieces in one by one. The water swallows them without a sound, the ripples spreading out slow.

I stand on the edge for a moment, the air cool against my skin, the city lights flickering in the distance.

Twenty-Two

The next couple of weeks is a haze, like living inside a strobe light—flashes of blood, cameras, moaning, and the metallic taste of danger that never fully dissolves. It feels like everything is on fire, and I'm the only one who doesn't want to put it out. The tabloids are eating me alive, splashing my face across every page, my name tumbling out of the mouths of people who don't know me but swear they do. The paparazzi are camped outside my building now, cameras clicking like a swarm of insects every time I leave, their voices a barrage of questions: *What are you wearing? Are you dating anyone? What happened to that guy who used to live with you?*

I don't even know which guy they're talking about but nevertheless I smile for them because this is what I wanted, what I bled for. This is the life.

It's harder to keep things clean now. There are more eyes on me, and some of them are too curious for their own good. Like the man who broke into my apartment last Friday, a fan, his face pale and sweaty, his breath hitching when he saw me. He told me he loved me, that he'd do anything for me, his words tumbling out in a flood of desperation that made my stomach churn and thrill at the same time.

I didn't scream. I didn't even flinch. I invited him in.

We drank wine on the couch, his hands trembling as he tried to hold the glass steady, his eyes darting to the curve of my neck, the way the fabric of my dress clung to my thighs. He told me his name, but I forgot it immediately.

When he leaned in, I let him, his lips clumsy and wet against mine, his hands fumbling at my waist. And then I pulled back, smiling, and told him to close his eyes.

He did, and that's when I swung.

The bat cracked against his head, the sound sharp and wet, and he crumpled to the floor like a bag of meat. Blood pooled around him, dark and glistening, and I stood over him, panting, my grip on the bat tight and steady. He wasn't dead—not yet.

I tied him to a chair, his arms limp, his head lolling to the side. When he came to, his eyes wild with fear, I laughed. It was the kind of laugh I hadn't heard from myself before—low, guttural, almost joyful.

I started with his fingers, snapping them one by one with pliers, the sound of bones breaking soft and satisfying. He screamed, his voice high and shrill, and it made the whole thing feel like a performance, like I was on set again. I used a cheese grater and scrubbed off the skin on his chest raw until the white meat showed, until he passed out from the pain. While he was passed out I took his tongue, pulling it from his mouth with the pair of pliers, the resistance of it thrilling, the blood pouring from his lips hot and metallic. He bled out almost immediately.

I stuck the tongue in the freezer, nestled between bags of ice and forgotten takeout, and went to bed. The next day, I pulled it out, its texture strange and firm, the frost clinging to its edges. I brought it back to my bed, let it thaw slightly in my hand, and slid it between my legs and masturbated with it. It was cold at first, sharp, but the thrill of it burned through me, the thought of him watching, the thought of my number one fan seeing me use his severed tongue as a sex toy. I feel like he would've died for this either way. I think of the cameras flashing, of the headlines that would follow if they knew what I was doing.

The next man was easier. He was a photographer, someone I'd met at a party a few nights earlier, his teeth too white, his hands too eager. I took him home, let him think he was in control, let him undress me slowly while I planned how to take him apart.

This time, I used a knife.

I carved into his chest first, shallow lines at first, just to watch him squirm. He begged, his voice cracking, his body shaking, but it only made me want to go deeper. By the time I was done, the floor was slick with his blood, my hands sticky, my dress ruined. I cut out his heart, held it in my hands, felt the last flicker of its beat before it stopped. I texted his wife a picture of my panties and told her he was running away with another woman.

The paparazzi are everywhere now. They chase my car through the streets, their lenses pressed against the glass of every restaurant, every club, every room I walk into. They shout my name like they own it, their flashes blinding, their questions relentless. But I don't run. I pose.

Alexa! Alexa! Alexa!

This is the life. This is what I killed for.

Every time I step outside, I feel them watching, feel the weight of their hunger, and it fills me with something warm and electric. I know it can't last. They'll catch me eventually, or the bodies will. But for now, I'm invincible.

Fame is a fire, and I want to burn with it until there's nothing left.

Twenty-Three

The set burns with light, so bright it feels like it's cooking me from the inside. It's the first day of filming the big movie with Shane West. The makeup chair smells like hairspray and plastic, the room humming with voices I can't quite make out. Ashleigh the makeup person is brushing powder onto my skin, her hands fast.

"You look perfect," she says.

The set feels fragile, as though the walls might fold inward if anyone speaks too loudly. The lights burn hot, blinding, stripping everything of shadow, but beneath it all is a hum, a vibration, a presence waiting to break through. My face is a mask, powdered smooth, lips painted just so. The reflection in the mirror doesn't blink back. The makeup artist murmurs something about perfection, but her hands are quick and mechanical, her voice hollow like she doesn't mean it.

The scene starts.

Shane West stands across from me, handsome in the way people expect him to be, his voice smooth as he says his lines. The space between us hums. I feel it rising in me, an itch in my throat, a tightening in my chest, a pressure pushing up and out. My jaw cracks open, wider than it should, and the sound of it echoes. The room falls silent.

The thing crawls out of me slowly, its movements jagged, like it's fighting the limits of flesh. Its body glistens, a slick, black mass of sinew and pulsing veins, as though it's been birthed from the darkest corner of the earth. Its arms stretch too long, almost boneless in the way they move, ending in claws that curve like the hooks. Its skin, if it can be called skin, ripples and shifts, mottled with sickly shades of gray and black that seem to swallow the light around it.

Its face—or the absence of one—is the worst. There are no eyes, only deep, hollow voids that seem to stare through me, through the walls, through the air itself. Its mouth is a jagged gash that runs too wide, stretching far beyond where its jaw should end, filled with teeth—rows and rows of them—like shards of shattered glass, glistening and sharp. They chatter as it moves, a sound like grinding bone, a sound that reverberates in the hollow of my chest. From the edges of its face spill long, writhing tendrils, slick and alive, curling in the air as if tasting it, reaching for something unseen.

The smell hits me next—something rancid, decaying, metallic. The air around it feels heavy, thick with the stench of blood and rot, and the sound of its breathing fills the room, low and wet, like the gurgling of water forced through something broken. As it drags itself free of me, my skin tears at the edges of my mouth, the pain sharp and hot, but I can't look away.

Its spine arches unnaturally, the ridges of its vertebrae pressing through its slick, glistening back like broken knives. Its movements are deliberate and wrong, each step jerky and uneven, as though it hasn't yet mastered the weight of its own form. And yet there's something elegant about it, something in the way it unfurls, like it's been waiting for this moment, savoring it.

When it fully emerges, it stands taller than any human should, its frame impossible, its presence consuming the space until it feels like there's no air left to breathe. It turns to face me, its eyeless voids locking onto mine, and I feel it—not in my head, but deeper, in the marrow of my bones, in the parts of me I didn't think could feel.

It opens its mouth, and the rows of teeth shift, grinding together, and I know, without it speaking, that it's smiling. "I love you Alexa." It speaks, low and guttural. Layered.

"I love you too." My heart swells. this is what real love feels like. This is my person.

It moves fast, crashing into Shane, its claws grabbing his head. He screams, a high, animal sound, his hands flailing at its chest, but the thing doesn't stop. Its fingers tighten around his skull, the flesh dimpling, cracking, until his head bursts with a sickening crunch. His eyes bulge first, popping out like overripe fruit, dangling by thin, glistening threads before they fall into the pool of blood spreading at his feet. The contents of his skull are a mess of thick, pink liquid, bubbling out in uneven globs, his brain collapsing into a wet, pulpy heap.

The thing tilts its head, inspecting the wreckage of Shane's face—or what's left of it—and then lowers itself to the body. Its claws grip the sides of the now-empty head, angling it as though positioning a camera, and then it thrusts in and out of his skull. The sound is wet and obscene, a sharp rhythm that echoes through the hollowed-out silence of the set. Shane's body jerks with each movement, limp and useless, the blood still pouring from his neck and pooling under the thing's knees. The smell of copper fills the room, thick and metallic, clinging to the back of my throat.

Someone screams—a sharp, panicked sound that breaks the spell—and the thing turns, its black eyes glinting. It pulls away from Shane's body, blood dripping from its claws, from its jagged edges, and lunges at the crew.

Joel, the grip, tries to run, but he catches him by the back of his neck, its claws sinking into his flesh. It tears his head clean off, the sound sharp and visceral, blood spraying in an arc across the cameras, the lights, the perfect white walls. It drops him the floor and punches a hole in his chest, splitting him open, his ribs cracking like dry branches. His insides spill onto the floor in wet, steaming clumps, his intestines trailing behind like ribbons.

Sarah, the assistant director, doesn't get far. She trips on a light cable, falling hard onto the floor, and he's on her before she can crawl away. It slashes through her back, splitting her spine, her screams choked off as blood fills her throat. It reaches his clawed hand down her throat and grabs her lungs, yanking them free from her mouth and hangs her from the rafters. Her body dangles, her eyes vacant and dead as she swings.

Margot, the production assistant, stands frozen, her hands pressed to her mouth, her body shaking. The thing grabs her by the throat, lifting her off the ground and scalps her clean, pulling her hair off like he's lifting a rug, the sound like wet Velcro. He throws her blonde hair to the side as her legs kick, her eyes wide and glassy, and the thing tilts its head, considering. As he tears through her middle I remember she brought her eight-year-old son to set. He tosses her into a light rig, her body convulsing as it is shocked with electricity. The sound of breaking glass is sharp and final.

The rest of the crew falls quickly. The thing moves through them, tearing, slashing, pulling them apart piece by piece. I almost cry out when it crushes Margots son's skull underfoot, the sound thick and wet, his brain splattering in uneven streaks across the floor. Poor boy never stood a chance. He didn't even try to run, just stayed cuddled up next to his mother's corpse, crying. It rips another person's jaw off, holding it up like a trophy before flinging it into the blood-slick walls.

When it's over, the set is a massacre. The walls are streaked with blood, the floor slick and sticky, the air heavy with the smell of copper, feces, and bile. The bodies are unrecognizable, broken and mangled, their limbs scattered, their faces obliterated. The lights flicker, their glow dimmed by the blood dripping from them, and the cameras stand still, their lenses cracked, their frames splattered.

End scene.

He turns to me, his black eyes endless, his body dripping with gore, its claws still twitching. He steps closer, his breath heavy and wet, the sound vibrating in my chest.

"We all rot eventually," he says, his voice a deep rumble, like stone grinding against stone.

I nod, my mouth still bleeding, my throat raw. "I know."

And I do. Because this was how it was always going to end.

I don't remember driving to the bridge. One moment I'm on set, standing in the ruins of bodies and blood, and the next I'm behind the wheel, the city lights flickering through the windshield. The bags under my eyes are dark, my hands sticky on the wheel, the smell of rot still clinging to my hair, my skin, my mouth.

The bridge looms ahead, its edges sharp against the night sky, and I don't slow down. The car hums beneath me, steady, patient, and I press the gas harder, the engine roaring in response.

I think about Ricky, about Two-Time Johnny, about the pieces of them sinking into the river, about the bodies I left behind on set, their blood still warm on my skin. I don't feel bad. Not for any of it.

The thing told me to do it, and I listened because it was right. We all rot eventually. We all fall apart. Why should I feel bad about trading blood for glory?

I hear sirens behind me, too many. Blue and red lights streaking across my face, and I start speeding. The car flies over the edge, the tires leaving the ground, the air rushing past me in a cold, sharp wave. For a moment, I'm suspended, weightless, the city of Los Angeles below me frozen in its bright, trembling vastness.

I close my eyes. I smile. I am famous. Alexa Valentine will be famous after this.

PROLOGUE

Breaking News: The Gruesome Secrets of Alexa Valentine Uncovered

In a shocking development, authorities have uncovered a grisly trail of evidence tying the late actress Alexa Valentine to a series of gruesome murders. Valentine, once a rising star known for her dramatic ascent to fame and controversial public image, is now suspected of killing at least fifty people over the last year.

Investigators were first tipped off after a routine welfare check at Valentine's West Hollywood condo revealed dismembered body parts hidden in freezers, closets, and under floorboards. The discovery sent shockwaves through the entertainment industry, which had long been fascinated by Valentine's meteoric rise and enigmatic persona.

The revelations took an even darker turn when authorities connected Valentine to the horrific carnage on the set of her last film, where multiple crew members were found brutally murdered. While Valentine had been initially dismissed as a victim of the chaos, a disturbing journal found among her belongings suggests a far more sinister explanation.

The journal, described by investigators as "profoundly disturbing," contains vivid and detailed accounts of Valentine's alleged possession by an "evil entity." In the entries, Valentine claims the entity promised her fame and adoration in exchange for a sacrifice—one she willingly offered. The sacrifice, according to the journal, was Lars Bauer, a former partner of Valentine's who died under mysterious circumstances months ago. His death marked the beginning of Valentine's horrifying descent.

One chilling entry reads: *"I told him I'd do it. The man in my mouth. I said his name out loud—Lars Bauer. The demon smiled inside me, its voice curling around my bones, promising everything I ever wanted. It told me fame needs blood, and I believed it. I believe it still."*

Investigators believe this entry was the catalyst for the wave of murders that followed, including the massacre on set, which survivors described as "otherworldly" in its brutality. Witness accounts of the on-set carnage describe Valentine behaving erratically in the days leading up to the incident, though none suspected the depths of the horrors she would unleash.

Valentine's life came to an abrupt and violent end two weeks ago when she drove her car off a cliff in Malibu the same night as the gruesome murders on set, the vehicle exploding on impact. While many hoped her death would bring answers, it has instead left more questions. Without Valentine alive to explain her actions, the journal serves as the only window into her mind—a mind seemingly gripped by something far beyond human comprehension.

Fans and critics alike are now divided on how to remember Valentine. Some insist she was a victim herself, manipulated by forces beyond her control, while others see her as a calculating killer who used the idea of possession as a twisted justification for her crimes.

As the entertainment world grapples with the fallout, one thing is certain: Alexa Valentine's story will not fade quickly. The actress who once craved the spotlight has become immortalized in infamy, her name forever tied to the blood-soaked legacy she left behind.

Authorities are continuing their investigation, though they warn the full extent of Valentine's crimes may never be uncovered. For now, Hollywood mourns not just the victims of her violence but also the chilling revelation that its brightest stars can sometimes burn the darkest.

Other works by the author include

Sugar

Shy Girl (Coming early 2025)

keep in contact with the author at:

Miaballardhorror.com
@galaxygrlmia on Instagram

Printed in Dunstable, United Kingdom